Kate & Frie

The Beginning

Emily McComiskey

self published using lulu.com

ISBN:978-1-387-90851-6

Please note that the events that seem unlikely to ever occur are intentional. None of my books are ever meant to make complete sense. 100% fiction

To say that something like what happened to me didn't happen or wasn't a real thing is a lie. So what if it happened so many years ago? I still remember it like it was like yesterday. I didn't ask for it to happen; no one asks for something like that to happen. No one thinks that they're going to face something like that. No one even thinks it's possible.

I was a senior in high school when it happened. I never dreamed that it'd be my school that day. I never dreamed that I'd be the one to see it start. Never did I think that I'd be the one who'd somehow be able to do what I managed to do. Never in my wildest dreams did I ever think that I'd have to fight for my life the way I had to then.

I guess I should start from the beginning. If I don't then most of my story wouldn't make sense. Well here it goes. Oh and I'm Kate by the way.

I was hanging out with my friends after school, just like always. We were sitting in my backyard; Kelly, May, and I that is. We were sitting under a tree trying to hide from the sun.

"How do you think you did on the test?" May asked. Her dark hair was pulled back in a ponytail; still hair stuck to the sides of her face.

Kelly shrugged "I dunno. It's not that big of a deal though if I didn't do too well. It's still the beginning of the year so I'd be able to keep my grades up even if this one turns out to be terrible." Her blonde hair was in a bun on the top of her head; curls lined the sides of her face. Somehow even in the heat her hair always looked great.

"Well do you think you at least passed?" I asked. My red hair was sticking to the sides of my face and the back of my neck. I had no way of doing anything about it; nothing would be able to tame my hair in this heat. I've learned from past experiences that tying my hair back in the heat wouldn't work; the elastic would break and I'd be stuck.

Kelly shrugged "I mean I think I passed but no one really knows if they do until they get their grade."

May rolled her eyes. "You do realize that you can ask teachers what your grade is before they hand it back right? Besides you get a message if you fail."

"Ever since the system crashed last year we only know if we've failed something though. We don't know what we've fail until we get it back." I said.

"I heard that they were working on that. I thought they fixed it." Kelly said.

I shook my head "They tried but they couldn't do it. They almost made it worse before they realized what they were doing."

"Oh hey! How's it going with your channel?" May asked.

I shrugged "I mean it could be better. It's not like it used to be. It's still popular but I don't really do much with it anymore. I'm thinking of just abandoning it."

"What?! Why? I thought you loved it. What happened to it that's making it less popular than it was?" Kelly asked.

I've always told them everything, they've always told me everything. What happened with the channel? That's something I haven't told them. I didn't think I could bring myself to tell them. The only person who knows is Steve, Mays twin brother. The fact that May doesn't already know is shocking. I would have thought she'd have been the first to know.

I shrugged "I dunno. I guess just like a lot of things; it was in the spotlight for a while and now the world has moved onto something else."

Neither of them believed me; I could tell by the looks on their faces. "You are aware of who your dad is right?" Kelly said.

I shot her a look. "I'm well aware of who my father is and at this moment in time I really don't care who he is. To me he'd always been my father. I don't know what he is anymore."

"I know it's tough for you with everything that's going on but please know that we're here for you. I know it's hard for you to adjust to it all." May said.

I started pulling at the grass beside me. "I guess it was only a matter of time until it happened. I just wish it didn't happen while I'm still in school. Everyone's now treating me differently because of who my father is."

"Have you talked to him about why he told everyone where he is and what he's been up to?" Kelly asked.

I shook my head. "I haven't; it's not like he's been here either. He was pulled away to do something. He didn't even get to explain to me what was going on. I really don't care anymore; he's not here and I don't know anything about it."

"Girls! Could all three of you come inside. The sprinklers are going to go off soon." Mom called from the back porch.

The three of us stood up, grabbed our bags and went inside. I closed the door once we were all inside. "Kelly and May, I know you're usually here for a few more hours but I'd like to talk with Kate. I think it'd be best for you both to head home." Mom said.

"Sure. Thanks for having us over again Jenna." Kelly said.

"No problem." May said.

They both grabbed their bags and left. Once the front door was closed Mom motioned for me to sit beside her on the couch. I sighed and sat next to her. "What do you want to talk to me about? I didn't do anything. And I don't want to talk about what Dad's up to." I said slightly annoyed.

Moms curly red hair was down, she must have been working from home today. Her brown eyes were soft and her pale skin was tinged pink. She must have been in the garden recently.

"Kate, I know you don't know what's going on and you blame your father for what's going on at school. Your father and I had no idea that anyone was told of where he was, what he's been up to or anything. Your father loves you very much; he wishes nothing but the best for you. You know that he left what he'd been doing so that you could grow up away from the problems your father and I both knew you'd face.

"We knew we couldn't keep you from it forever; we wanted to keep you away from it until you were mature and ready to handle it. We had no plans to tell anyone outside the family of where we are until you left college. The family knows what we wanted for you; they all knew and promised not to tell anyone. I know that it was not anyone in our family who let it slip.

"I know you blame him for it but please give him a chance to talk with you. You know who he really is and if he could, he'd still be here with us."

I was staring at my feet, I really didn't want to talk about him. "I don't get why he was pulled away. I mean I know that he's a writer, he always has been. But why would he be pulled away now that people know where he's been?"

Mom sighed "He was pulled away because he had done something he shouldn't have done.. When he and I found out that we were having you we packed up and left. No one knew that your father had been writing those books. You know he uses a different name for his books.

"Well his publishers wanted him to reveal who he really is. It was in his contract that at some point he'd have to come clean and tell everyone who he is. As you know we were already together when your fathers books started taking off. We were both getting ready for him to reveal himself. When we found out about you; we couldn't go back and push it off. We tried but we couldn't; we just couldn't do it.

"We agreed that it'd be best for you to grow up away from people following your father. We didn't know what was going to happen once it was made public. We were prepared to face it together but we weren't prepared to face it with a baby.

"You father was pulled away because he now has to go talk with his publishers. They weren't happy when they found out that he was nowhere to be found. They did eventually find him; your dad told them that he'd keep writing but only if they wouldn't reveal who he is until he made the call. We had to pay them back for the marketing they put into it originally before they agreed.

"Now that it's out he had to go back and work everything out with them. He never made this public and he doesn't know who did. He's not happy about it because he knows what you're facing in school. He didn't want you to go through this."

"So? He's supposed to be my father before anything else. He promised me that he'd continue the family tradition and now he can't because of all this." I was acting like a child.

"I know that you're upset with the way everything turned out. Please, don't take it out on your father. He really did try his best."

I huffed. "If he'd tried his best then he'd be here with us instead of wherever the hell he went." I didn't pay attention to where he had gone.

"Kate, please. Just talk with him. He has to do this. If he doesn't then it'll be worse than it is now. Just call him, please."

I moaned "I rather not."

"How would you feel if you didn't talk with him and something happened?"

"I'd be happy because then it means he got what he deserves."

"I know you don't mean that."

I rolled my eyes. I got up, went upstairs and to my room. I slammed the door behind me. I sat at my desk and turned on my computer. Might as work on editing my video.

I must have spent two hours on my computer before I fell asleep. I awoke to my phone ringing beside my ear. I blinked a few times and answered. "Hello?" I mumbled.

"Hey Kate. You talking to me now?" Dad said.

I now realized that I had answered the phone for my father. "I didn't realize who was calling me. Now that I know it's you I regret my choice." I snapped.

"Kate, you know that-" I cut him off by hanging up. I expected him to call me back but he didn't.

I stood up and got into bed. I was quickly once again sleeping.

"Kate Marie Williams!" Mom shouted as she opened my door the next morning.

I moaned "I didn't do anything."

She pulled the blankets off me and pulled me to my feet. She held onto my shoulders with a firm grip. "How dare you speak to your father the way you did last night! We raised you better than this!"

It took me a moment to register what she was talking about. "So? He's not my father anymore." I said.

"He is your father and you know it. Stop acting like a brat! Get ready for school or you'll miss your buss. Don't go back to sleep." She walked out of my room closing the door behind her.

I huffed and got ready for school. Ten minutes later I was in the kitchen. I grabbed my lunch money off the counter and turned to head towards the front door.

"Kate, I'm sorry I yelled at you this morning. I just hope you realize what you're doing. Have fun at school today."

I grunted in response as I walked out the front door. I walked down the driveway and down the street. I stood at the corner waiting for the bus.

"Hey Kate. How are you doing this morning?" May said joining me at the bus stop.

I huffed and shrugged. "I hate going to school. I hate my father. I hate my mother. I hate my life. Everything's just dandy."

"Sorry to hear that. I didn't think you'd be so upset over everything. I get the feeling that this isn't just about your dad. You've been off before he left."

I threw my hands up in the air. "Why would you think that anything has been 'off' before my father left? It's not like any bullshit has been going on before then!" I shouted.

"You and Steve have both been off since before this all started. I don't know what you two aren't talking about or what you are; I'd really like to know why the two of you aren't the same anymore! Look I know you're upset with a lot of things but something happened before everything with your dad and you're not talking about it. What could you possibly be keeping from everyone that only Steve would know. Whatever it is he won't tell me and neither will you. Kelly doesn't seem to know either and I"d like to know what's bothering my best friend!" May shouted.

"You really want to know? You sure about wanting to know?" I snapped.

"Yes! Of course I want to know what's bothering you!" She shouted.

"Steve is a complete ass and I never should have dated him. I can't believe I let you talk me into that!" I shouted.

Her face went from light pink, to bright red, to ghostly pale in a matter of seconds. "Kate, I'm so sorry. I didn't know."

"Well now you know and I'd really prefer it if you leave me the hell alone. Besides you'd just take his side so might as well cut you out of my life as well." I snapped.

The bus pulled up to the curb and opened the door. I climbed up the steps and sat in the back of the bus in an empty seat. I didn't bother to look to see where May sat.

When the bus got to school everyone got off and went inside. I walked through the front door and instantly people stopped talking to look at me. I put my head down and went to the library. I sat in the back corner and started reading.

"You okay Kate?" Someone asked.

I looked up and saw the school librarian standing in front of me. Her black hair was in braids, around her neck she work a small metal book.

I shrugged "I'm okay Mrs. Z."

She pulled over a chair from a nearby table and sat. "I've gotten to know you over the past three, almost four years of you being here. I think I know you well enough to say that something really is bothering you." Her voice was kind and gentle.

"You've known me longer than almost four years. You've known me since I was in preschool."

"I may have met you then but I also know who you are now. I know what you were like when you were in preschool and I know what you're like now."

I gave her a small smile "How can you always make me smile when I'm here?" I asked.

She laughed a little. "I'm not too sure. I want you to know that; well I'll tell you what, come see me at the end of the day. I have something I want to give you."

I was confused. "Okay?"

"You better get ready to head out of here, the bell is about to ring."

No sooner had she finished speaking did the bell ring. I picked up my bag, threw it over my shoulder and headed towards the door. I turned my head back towards Mrs. Z "Have a nice day." I said.

"You as well." she replied.

I pushed open the door and headed down the hall. As I walked everyone was staring at me; it made me uneasy. Why shouldn't I feel uneasy when the whole school is staring at me all the time now.

I was tripped twice, pushed down multiple times, pushed on purpose multiple times and was even pulled backwards a few times. By the time I reached my locker I'd had enough and just wanted to go home. There was a sign on my locker that read: Why don't you run away like your dad did. I tore it off, ripped it up and threw it into my locker. I slammed my locker shut and went to class.

At lunch I hid in the library and read my book. Mrs. Z. was lecturing students who were trying to put gum on the computers. When lunch was over I went to my last class and sat in the back of the room. I've been sitting in the back of all my classes. I've even been hiding in the locker room during gym.

When the final bell rang I gathered my things and hurried to the library. I opened the door and walked over to Mrs. Z's desk.. "Hey, how was your day?" Mrs. Z. asked; coming out of the back room.

I shrugged "Well no one dumped anything on my head today; which is good. But still today wasn't anything like I'd rather be in."

"Well, if you're in one piece and clean then I'd say today was a good day."

I smiled "I guess you're right."

She picked up a flash drive from the desk and handed it to me. "I've been working on this for a few weeks. I figured you'd need someone to remind you of a few things. I hope you enjoy it."

"Oh. You didn't have to. I'd have been fine without it. I'd never ask you to go to the trouble of doing something for me."

She smiled "I normally don't do this type of thing. The flash drive will explain why. You better hurry or you'll miss your bus."

I took the flash drive, smiled and hurried out the door. I hurried out of the school and to the bus. I'd just made it to the bus. I hurried onto it and sat in the first empty seat I could find; meaning I sat behind the bus driver.

I stared out the window; not uttering a word until the bus arrived at my stop. The doors opened and I got off. Instead of waiting on the sidewalk for May like I usually do; I sprinted down the sidewalk towards my house. I pulled out my key, unlocked the door, went inside, slammed it behind me and ran up the stairs to my room.

I pulled the flash drive from my bag and put it into my computer. Once the computer registered the drive I opened it and saw it contained two folders; they were labeled *one* and *two*. I opened the one labeled one and saw it contained many images. I didn't want to sit there and go through them all so I went back and opened the other one. Inside was only a single file; a video. I clicked on it and it started to play.

I quickly realized what the video was. It contained images of when I was younger; I stopped it and took out the flash drive. I threw it into my desk and pulled out my homework. I didn't know what she was trying to do and I wasn't going to watch the video to find out.

I worked in silence; my phone rang a few times but I didn't answer it. When I finished I went down to the basement. Normally I don't go to the basement; it's only full of boxes. I'd much rather be upstairs using my computer, watching tv, or reading. I came down to the basement because I wanted to hide something; I no longer wanted it. I wanted to hide it somewhere where I knew my parents would find it at some point. I knew that by hiding it down here they weren't going to find it for a long time.

I turned on the light and walked around; I wanted to find a box they rarely ever go in to put it in. I went to the back corner and searched for a box. I found a box that had a fading label and dust all over it. I took the boxes on top of it off and put them on the floor. I opened the box and moved the cover to the side.

I reached around my neck and took off my necklace. I held it in my hand; I ran my thumb over the small heart I held in my palm. I could feel the carvings on my thumb as it moved across the surface.

I lifted something in the box onto its side and put the necklace into the box; it fell to the bottom. I placed the object back down and put the cover on. I put the boxes back on top and headed towards the stairs. I turned off the light and went upstairs. I went back to my room closing the door behind me. I sat on my bed and read my book.

I heard Moms car pull into the driveway later that evening. She had been working late so we'd be eating whatever we found in the house. I had a sandwich an hour ago.

"Kate! Could you please come down here?" Mom called. I knew she was at the bottom of the stairs.

I huffed but went downstairs. "What's up? Please tell me that we aren't talking about Dad again."

She shook her head. "No we're not talking about him tonight. I wanted to ask you what happened at school. Did anything happen today?"

I shrugged "I mean nothing was dumped on me but I was still picked on. Other than that nothing happened."

She sighed "What did they do today?"

I shrugged "Just pushing me around and stuff. Please don't do anything. I don't need to be picked on anymore than I already am."

She sighed "I rather do something about it than just sit to the side and allow it to happen. Is that all that happened today?"

I stared blankly at her; I knew she already knew. "I know you know what else happened today so no nothing else happened today." I snapped.

She folded her arms across her chest. "Why didn't you tell me that you guys broke up? Why are you pushing Kelly and May away?"

I rolled my eyes "Well lets see; Steve's an ass so I really don't give a damn. May is his sister but also was a good friend. Kelly's just oblivious to a lot of things."

"I'm asking you to not push your friends away. I know you feel like you can handle this on your own but trust me, you can't. You can't go through this on your own. Your friends are there for you even when you don't want them to be."

I huffed "How would you know? I doubt you've had any problems when you were my age."

"You know that's not true. My life isn't perfect nor has it ever been."

I rolled my eyes and huffed. "I'll believe it when I see it. You say you've struggled when you were my age but guess what! You were adopted and your parents weren't living two lives!"

"Kate-"

"NO! Just stop trying to be here for me and let me go through this alone. I rather do this alone because I am alone!" I snapped. I ran from the kitchen, up the stairs and to my room; I slammed the door behind me.

I fell onto my bed and started crying. My phone rang several times; I pushed it away and it fell to the floor. I curled up in a ball and went to sleep.

Come December I was no longer the same person I wanted to be; I was no longer who I've always been. I stopped doing my homework, I stopped eating, I no longer talked with anyone; not even Mrs. Z. When I was at home with Mom all I ever did was fight with her.

I haven't spoken to my father since I accidentally answered his call. He still wasn't home and I no longer cared. Let him do whatever it was he's doing. If he really cared about me then he'd be here instead of wherever he was.

I was walking back to class when I saw someone in the halls. Sure it wasn't unusual to see people in the halls during the day. But this person was different; he was a fully grown man and not someone who worked at the school.

I saw something in his jacket reflect light from the ceiling. I sucked in air and wanted to scream. Someone put their arm around me and put something against my throat. I quickly realized what was going on. I screamed and the knife against my throat started to turn.

A nearby teacher heard me scream and came out into the hall. "Hey! Let her go!" the teacher shouted. They pushed me to the floor and went after the teacher. I slowly got to my feet and watched in horror as the teacher was stabbed to death. I started screaming and took off running.

I ran to the end of the hall and into the first classroom that had an open door. "THERE'S ARMED PEOPLE IN THE SCHOOL!" I shouted upon entering the classroom.

Everyone started to panic. Everyone was gathering up their things so they could get out. There was a loud explosion and the school shook.

The ceiling started to crumble and quickly came crashing down. I was hit on the head by something and fell to the floor. I felt blood start to fall from where I'd been hit. Something else fell from above and hit my head. I blacked out.

I came around sometime later. I was buried under debris from the second floor caving it. One arm was free, I started to pull stuff off myself. I got my other arm free and began to attempt to pull the heavier stuff off. No matter how much I tried I couldn't do it. I couldn't move anything; not to mention my arms were covered in cuts and hurt like crazy.

I started crying. I cried because I was scared, alive, in pain, and for how I'd been acting. Tears fell from my eyes and quickly caused pain; I could only assume that I had cuts under my eyes.

I couldn't shift my position; there was no way I could since I was under so much debris and only my arms were free. I couldn't feel anything on my body. I only felt pain; I had no clue if I still had my legs or not.

I heard someone running in the halls; they were getting closer. "Are you okay?" They asked as they knelt down.

"Ohhh totally! I'm only under hear because I can get myself out." I said sarcastically.

They huffed. "You've got to be pretty upset if you're saying that right now."

I turned my head slightly to the right to see who it was. I huffed when I saw Steve. "Why does it have to be you?"

"Haha very funny. Do you want to get out of there or not?"

I stared blankly at him "Nooo I want to stay in here and die." I was shocked at the amount of truth was there.

He pushed himself onto his feet and starting moving things. "Just so you know it wasn't what I said that got you pissed off."

"Ya right. If it wasn't you then why did it come from your phone."

He huffed and threw something. "My friends can be assholes."

"Which friends? The ones who are really your friends or the ones who just say that."

Again he threw something before he spoke. "The ones who only said that. I hope you know that I didn't know they were doing that. I flipped out when I saw them with my phone. I didn't know they had it and I didn't know they were able to get in. I don't know what they found on there. I didn't even know they texted that to you until you weren't answering me."

"Oh so then you know what they told me? Because last I checked I didn't tell you what was sent to my phone."

He sighed "I found out because I took your phone and went through the messages between us."

"You took my phone?! When did you do that!"

"When you were hanging out in the backyard with May a while back. You didn't have it because you left it on the coffee table."

"Glad to know you know how to break into my phone." I snapped.

"It's not breaking in if you know the password."

"It still isn't your phone to begin with."

"True but I didn't really think about that. I just wanted to know why you were mad at me."

"How wonderful. I'm glad to know that you take things that don't belong to you."

"By the way in case you're blaming everything going on with your dad on me; I didn't tell anyone."

"I wasn't blaming that on you. I've been blaming my dad for it. He's the only one who can make that call and everyone says it came from him."

"I dunno. Your dad doesn't seem like the kind of person who'd do that. I don't know everything about why he was doing that but I really don't think he would do that to you."

"I dunno."

"I'm going to attempt to move this and when I do I want you to try and pull yourself out from under it. Do you think you can do that?"

"I guess."

He grunted as he lifted the bookshelf off my legs. I suddenly felt light headed. I wanted to pass out but I knew I couldn't. I used my hands to pull myself away.

I moaned in pain as I slid across the floor. He dropped the bookshelf once I was out; it landed with a loud crash. He held his hands out in front of him to help me to my feet.

"I dunno if I can stand. I can't really feel my legs right now." I said as I took his hands. I leaned forward and sat up. I tried to get to my feet but nope; couldn't do it. I shook my head "Nope can't do it."

Steve sighed "You're going to hate this."

I moaned, I knew what he was talking about and I knew that I needed help. "I have no choice."

He crouched down into a squat. He put one arm around my back and the other under my knees. As he stood up I put my arms around his neck, I didn't want to fall. He walked at a steady pace down the empty halls.

I felt dizzier than I had been originally; I felt as though I was going to pass out. I leaned my head against his shoulder so my head wouldn't fall backwards and cause anymore pain. I doubted I'd feel the pain if I passed out. Either way I didn't want my head to fall backwards, I'd look like I was dead if my head was tilted back.

Once outside I squinted due to the snow reflecting the sunlight. I couldn't hear many people around; I assumed everyone had left. Well, everyone who was alive. I didn't know who died and who didn't.

My mind started racing with all the possibilities of what happened to May. Kelly wasn't in school today since she had left last night to go see her family for the holidays. May was in school; she was always in school. I didn't know what happened to her and I wanted to know.

"I know you're not talking with May but she's okay. She was able to hide until it was over. She's around here somewhere; where exactly I don't know but I know she's okay."

I couldn't respond; I wanted to but I didn't have the energy. I was starting to hear people talking and sirens. I had my eyes closed; I couldn't hold them open anymore.

"OH MY GOD! KATE!" May shouted.

"Where was she? Is she alive? The police did a search of the school twice and didn't see her! How could they have missed her? Is she aware of what you're doing?" May was panicking.

"She's alive. She was under a pile of debris from when the first bomb went off. She was aware of what was going on around her when I found her. I think that when I took the bookshelf off was when she wasn't really aware of what's going on. She was at first but even then it was confusing."

"The school called her mom three and a half hours ago to tell her that they couldn't find her and she was most likely dead. It ended four hours ago."

"May I know. She needs to be taken to a hospital. Why don't you call her mom, tell her that Kate's alive."

"Uhh I hope you know that you're doing that. You're also taking the car and following us to the hospital. I'm going with her."

"Whatever."

I heard people running before I blacked out again.

My eyes were closed; I was starting to become aware of what's around me. I really wasn't sure of where I was until I heard the beeping of machines. I knew I was in the hospital when I heard the beeping. I moaned and forced my eyes open.

I was temporarily blinded by the lights in the room. Slowly my eyes adjusted and I was able to see the fuzzy outlines of things around me. After a few minutes I was able to see clearly. I looked around, I was definitely in the hospital. I searched for any indication of where I was. I found a window to my right, I looked out and quickly realized that I wasn't in any hospital near home; I was in a Boston hospital.

I could hear the sounds of the city outside and the faint noises of people walking in the halls. I was relieved that I'm still alive but I had a pit in my stomach. No sooner had I realized that I'm alive did guilt wash over me. Guilt for how I'd been treating everyone.

The door opened and I turned to see who came in. I smiled and shouted "Dad!"

He smiled and came over to me. He put his arms around me and I put my arms around him; well the best I could. "I'm so sorry baby girl. I love you very much." He whispered into my ear.

"I love you too Dad."

He pulled away, pulled a chair to the side of the bed and sat. He played with his ring, he was nervous. He always played with his ring when he got nervous. "We thought you died. No one found you; no one knew where you were. Your Mom, she called me to tell me but she couldn't speak. We have no idea how you ended up here or anything. We're both happy you're alive." his voice cracked a few times as he spoke.

"I'm sorry I wouldn't talk with you."

He gave me a small smile "I know baby girl. I know you've been out cold the past few days but do you know anything that happened?"

"What do you mean?"

His voice was soft "Do you remember what happened on the twenty third while you were at school?"

"I thought that it was a dream! It really happened?"

Dad nodded "It really happened. Do you remember where you were and how you got here?"

I closed my eyes, trying to remember. "Well I was on my way back to class when I saw someone in the hall. He wasn't a student nor a teacher. Someone grabbed me and put something against my neck. I screamed; a teacher came into the hall and told them to leave me alone. I was pushed to the floor and they went towards the teacher. The teacher was stabbed to death. I took off running and screaming. I ran into a classroom, said something, heard an explosion and the next thing I know is I'm here. I really thought it was just a dream."

Dad was silent for a while, still he played with his ring. "Do you know what they looked like?"

I shook my head, pain shot down my back. "No, I only remember that I saw two guys."

He sighed and didn't say anything.

"Where's Mom? Wouldn't she have come with you?"

"She'll be here soon. I couldn't get a flight until last night. When the plane landed I took the bus over here. She knows I was going to take the bus and come here." He looked at his watch "She'll let me know when she gets here. You know how she is when she has to drive in the city."

I smiled "I know. She doesn't say a word and jumps when her phone goes off."

Dad smiled, his smile quickly faded. "Kate, I know you've been upset with me. I know I promised you that I'd continue the family tradition with you and I haven't been able to. I just wish -"

"I know what you're trying to say. I shouldn't have acted the way I have been. It's just, I've always had you around. I've always had it in my head that you're my dad; I wanted you to just be with me and Mom. I'm sorry that I've overreacted."

"I would have been surprised if you didn't get upset. Kate, I did what I did because I've always wanted the best for you. There's nothing in this world that would keep me from being here for you. I'm the one who failed, not you.

"I know I didn't explain everything to you beforehand and I should have. I had to leave because if I didn't then I don't know what could have happened. I had to take care of it."

"I get now why you had to go. I guess that even though I'm not ready; we're never going to be left alone again."

He gave me a small smile. "Yes and no. I'm never going to be left alone; you however will be left alone far more than your mom and I." He leaned forward and hugged me.

"I love you baby girl. No matter what you'll always be my little girl."

I smiled "Thanks Daddy."

"I thought you said you weren't going to call me that anymore; you said you were too old for it."

"For the most part yes; but right now I need you like a little girl needs her father."

"I hope you know I'm always going to be here for you."

"I know. Even when I want to push you away, you'll always be my favorite person to go to. Well you and Mom."

He chuckled "I'd much rather have you come to us instead of staying away."

I smiled.

"Shaun, is she okay?" Mom said.

He sat back and looked at Mom "I'd say she's still our little girl." a smile played across his face.

Mom put her hand across her heart and smiled. "Kate, are you okay?"

"I'm okay Mom. Do you know how I ended up here?"

She shook her head as she walked towards me. She bent down and wrapped her arms around me. "I don't really know to be honest. I was working from home; so like normal when I took my lunch break I watched a little tv. The news was on and I saw the school flash across the screen. I saw what a camera in the parking lot had; parts of the school blew up. I tried calling you and texting you; I couldn't reach you. I had no idea where you were or what happened to you. Once it ended the school called to say they couldn't find you." She shook her head; Dad took her hand and rubbed his thumb against the back of her hand.

"The hospital called me to tell me you were here. I called your mother to tell her. We've both been terrified; we didn't know what was going to happen. We still don't know everything that happened." Dad said.

"Did she tell you something?" Mom mumbled.

Dad nodded "I'll tell you later, I promise."

Mom nodded and wiped tears from her face.

"I'm sorry for how I've been acting Mom."

She gave me a small smile; one that quickly faded. "I know; I know it's been hard for you. That doesn't matter to me right now. I'm more concerned about what's going to happen now."

"Does anyone know what happened at the school?" I asked.

Mom and Dad shared a look. "Well as you know there was a time when such things weren't often heard of. For some reason such events started happening more and more. They have many ideas around why it became so common. Now that they've started to really take action and put more into the safety of public spaces such events have gone down. No one knows how they were able to get into the school or how they were able to have more than the two of them involved. There's a lot that is still unknown." Dad said.

I sighed "It doesn't make sense though. It's a small town school!"

"We know that. Everyone knows that. I wish we could answer all your questions; we just can't right now." Mom said.

I sighed "I know, it bugs me though."

"I know." Mom said.

"Dad, do you have to go back?"

"Not right now. At some point I will, for now I'm going to be here. You guys mean more to me than anything. I'd kick myself for going anywhere. I already am kicking myself for leaving you guys in the first place."

"Even though we weren't the same the past few months; we knew you'd come home when you could." Mom said.

"I knew you'd come home but I didn't know when and that's what scared me." I said.

Dad smiled and shook his head. "I know this isn't the ideal place to be this time of year and everything, I'm just glad that we're all together."

I started to feel light headed and dizzy, I didn't understand. I thought I was going to be fine! I wanted to scream but I couldn't, I couldn't move.

"Kate are you okay?" Both my parents asked.

I wanted to say something to them but I couldn't, I couldn't even shake my head to give them an answer.

My eyes sprang open, my head was pounding, my heart was racing and my face felt as though it was on fire. The machines around me were beeping. I moaned in pain. I wanted to go home; I no longer wanted to be here.

I heard someone in a chair nearby; I lifted my head slightly to see who it was. My head went up before quickly going back down, I was able to see a glimpse of who it was, Dad was asleep in a chair in the corner, Mom was nowhere in sight.

"How ya doing?" Dad mumbled; he sounded as though he hadn't slept for a while.

"I dunno, I dunno what happened. What's going on?"

I heard him sigh as he shifted his position. "I don't really know, doctors aren't too sure either. Whatever it is, it's affecting your spin more than anything else. Your legs and arm healed just fine. Something is going on with your spin that's not allowing it to heal like it should."

I felt tears form in the corners of my eyes, I blinked a few times, I didn't want to cry, not now. "What do you mean my arms and legs healed up just fine? I don't have the casts on anymore?"

"Right, you no longer have the casts on."

"Then why am I still here?"

"They're not going to send you home until they know what's going on with your spin. Kate-" he sighed "I really don't want to tell you this but I have no choice." he sighed again "Kate, sometimes you end up having a seizure, they come out of nowhere.. Always unexpected, never predictable and always scaring Mom and I."

I sighed "How much time has passed?"

Dad appeared at the side of the bed, he sat on the edge and put his hand on top of mine. "Five months."

"Have I been sleeping the whole time?"

He avoided my eyes; he was scared. "Under the doctors control yes."

"Mom's at work isn't she" I mumbled. I hated seeing him scared. I didn't want him to worry about me more than he already was.

He nodded "You know she'd be here if she could. She just can't take a whole lot of time off from the office. She does her best."

24

"I know. She has to keep working even though this happened. Has anyone tried to come besides you and Mom?"

Again he avoided making eye contact. "May and Kelly keep trying, they're not allowed. Steve tried once, I almost beat the crap out of him."

My eyes grew wide; something had just click in my head. What had just clicked, I had a vague idea and I knew exactly who I had to talk to, no matter what.

"You okay?" Dad asked; his voice filled with concern.

I nodded "Ya, I'm fine. Dad, you're not going to like this; I need to talk with May and Kelly and Steve."

His face went rigid "why?" was all he said.

"You'll see."

"Kate, I'm not letting them come here to see you if you won't tell me."

"Then I guess I'll have to do something else. I'm not going to tell you, not just yet."

He eyed me with suspicion, he knew I was up to something. What can I say, I'm definitely up to something now. I smiled at my father "Please trust me on this. I don't want you to keep worrying about me."

"I'm always going to worry about you. And the fact that you're asking me to trust you on this doesn't help. Too much like me. I'd say."

I laughed "I know. I'm just like you, mischievous."

"At the same time you have Moms common sense. There's a reason my parents refused to answer a lot of your questions when you were little."

"Because you were always, in their minds, too stupid with what you were doing. Although you never did anything illegal or drugs."

He started laughing "You're completely right my little one."

"How ya doing Kate?" Mom asked as she walked towards me.

"I'm okay. I thought you had to go to work."

She studied my face and sighed. "What on earth are you planning? Kate, please don't get anymore wild ideas until you're out of here."

"I'm my fathers daughter with my mothers common sense." I said.

"What the heck does that mean?"

I smirked "At the moment nothing. When it's going to mean something, I really have no clue."

She sighed "Shaun what is she talking about?"

"Beats me. She woke up maybe an hour ago; so I highly doubt that anyone has any idea what's going on in her head right now. Besides she still doesn't have a phone."

Three weeks passed and I was able to go home. I guess the reason I was able to leave after being awake for three weeks is because of what the doctors had done while they were keeping me asleep. I don't know what they were doing and because I'm able to walk, I don't really mind not knowing. Maybe someday day I'd like to know, but not right now.

I got a new phone, thankfully everything that was on my phone before came back. I have yet to look to see if there's anything on there that could help, I've been too nervous.

I jumped off the stairs and slid into the wall. "I'm okay." I quickly said.

"Why don't you not do that for a while, just for now." Dad said.

I smiled "I know, just hard to remember. Hey can I go out?"

"Depends, where would you be going and with who."

"Oh I'd just be going to the park, I guess I'd just be walking around for a while. Maybe see if Kelly and May are willing to meet up with me."

He eyed me suspiciously "Would Steve be meeting up with you as well?"

I shook my head "No, he won't talk to me. So can I go?" I was lying, Steve had talked to me, once.

"Well I don't see why you can't go. Just let me know what you're up to. How are you going to get there? You haven't been cleared by the doctor to drive yet."

I shrugged "I know, I was planning on walking."

"Okay. Which park?"

"The one near the school, it's close by all of us."

"Which one there's five."

"The one down the street from the high school."

"Okay. Let me know when you get there please."

"I know." I opened the door "See ya later."

He smiled "Be home in time for dinner."

"I will." I promised. I walked through the door, closing it behind me. I walked down the front walk and down the side of the road.

I took my time, I wanted to enjoy the late spring weather. As usual in New England the weather is unpredictable; today it's a warm sunny day, it wasn't humid, and clouds dotted the sky above. Tomorrow could easily be a hot, humid and rainy day, it's been known to happen but not always. I took my time to enjoy the weather, today is just one of those days where you really want to be outside and doing things. Today is one of the days where you just want to be outside even if all you want to do is be inside.

I crossed the street and walked through the small parking lot for the park. I walked down the hill, across the grass and onto the bridge. Even though it's made of cement you can see where the sun hits most.

I stood in the middle, near the edge. I looked at the surrounding trees, the sky above and the river below. I smiled at how beautiful it looked. The water looked blue despite the normal coloring of brown. The sky was bright with only a few small clouds. The tree branches were filled with leaves overlooking the river below. I pulled my phone out of the back pocket of my shorts, I slid the screen to the left and took a picture.

I was about to put my phone away when it vibrated, Kelly texted me. I opened my phone and read the message. *May & I r on the way. Sorry if we're late.* I smiled and shook my head in amusement. I sent her the picture I just took, *That's ok. I have this to keep me busy rn.* She quickly sent a laughing emoji. I turned my phone off and put it in my pocket.

No one was here besides myself, despite it being mid morning. I could hear cars speeding up and down the road. I heard something that caught my attention, I turned too search for the noise. I watched as a car slowed down and pulled into the small parking lot.

The car pulled into a space near the trees, the lights went out and the door opened, Steve got out. He closed the door and started walking down the hill.

Another car pulled in, and parked. May and Kelly appeared on either side of the car. They closed the doors and ran down the hill. I took off running towards them. I ran into them and put one arm around each of them, they each put an arm around me as well.

"I've missed you guys." I said.

"We've been really worried about you." Kelly said.

"We're glad you're out of the hospital now." May said.

I pulled away and stood in front of them smiling, my smile quickly faded. "May were you hurt?" I asked.

She shook her head. "No, I was able to hide, no one found me until it was over. I was terrified, I didn't know what was going on or what was going to happen."

"I'm glad you didn't get hurt."

"Me too."

"Kelly what about you?" I asked.

"I wasn't even there. When I found out, I passed out. I couldn't believe it. I wanted to call you both but I didn't until I heard that they were searching the school for the second time. I called you first, it rang like crazy for a few seconds before dropping the call. I called May and she answered right away. We thought you were dead."

"Well I'm alive."

Kelly shrugged "Yeah, but you almost did die."

I started choking on air "What?" I said as I stopped coughing.

"You didn't know?" May asked.

I shook my head "I didn't, I do now."

"Steve how did you get here first?" May asked.

I barely acknowledged that he was now standing with us.

"I left before you. You went to get Kelly and while I didn't make any stops." Steve said. "So why did you want us all here?" He asked.

"Well I want to know what happened. I know how it started, I think but I don't know how I got the injuries I had, nor do I know how I ended up at the hospital. I have a vague idea, I think it's too insane to even be real."

The three of them shared a look; they all seemed to have an unspoken agreement. "You don't remember?" May asked slowly.

I shook my head "No. All I remember is that I was leaving the bathroom and I saw someone with something behind their back. Someone put their arms around me and put a knife or something against my throat. I screamed, a teacher came out and told them to leave me alone. They dropped me and stabbed the teacher to death. I took off running and next thing I know I wake up in the hospital."

"You had a knife to your throat!" Kelly screamed.

29

"Yes. I didn't ask for you guys to come here to go over what I remember. I want to know what happened that I don't remember." I was slightly annoyed.

Again the three of them shared a look. "Steve's the one who knows. He's said very little about what he knows; drives me insane." May said.

"I've told you that I don't have to tell you everything." Steve said, annoyed.

May rolled her eyes "I would have thought you'd have the decency to tell me why the hell you were carrying her out the school! I would love to know where you found her and what happened!" she shot back.

"WHAT?!" I shouted.

May sighed and took several deep breaths; not uttering a word.

"You were aware of your surroundings; you're the one who told me what you've now forgotten." Steve said.

"Why is he even here? I thought you only wanted to talk with May and I."

"I'd like to know why as well. I never said a word to him about this. I didn't even know he knew until he offered me a ride." May said.

I folded my arms across my chest. "I know you guys didn't know. I asked him to come, I didn't mention him because I wanted to avoid another world war. Clearly I failed."

"Why didn't he mention it before then? You sent those messages three days ago." May snapped.

"I dunno! I never said he couldn't say anything to you!" I shouted.

"You're the one who broke up with him!" she snapped.

"Wait; I thought-"

"Bud out!" I shouted at Kelly. "It's not my fault you wanted us to go out! I told you I was against it!" I screamed.

"SO?! I could see the way you looked at him!"

"ONE TIME! ONE FREAKIN TIME AND YOU GET THAT MESSAGE!"

"LIES!"

"HE'S AN ASSHOLE AND YOU KNOW IT!"

"ASSHOLE AND PAIN ARE DIFFERENT! HE'S MY BROTHER SO I'M STUCK WITH HIM NO MATTER WHAT!"

"I DON'T GIVE A DAMN! STOP STICKING UP FOR ASSHOLES THEN COME FIND ME!" I turned on my heel and took off running.

I ran towards the bridge, I'd cut through the woods to get home. I didn't want anyone to see me if I started crying before I got home

I was halfway to the bridge when someone grabbed my wrist. I pulled away and briefly turned my head to see who it was. I scowled and sped up.

Steve grabbed my arm and stopped running, I was still running. I was pulled backwards and had no choice but to face him. "What the hell do you want?" I spat.

"I know I'm not your favorite person and I probably never was. I know that you and May have always been good friends. I didn't see why you guys stopped talking, I don't know what happened to you guys. You may think that we're all going to be able to share what we know like nothing has happened; it doesn't work that way and it's not going to."

I rolled my eyes. "What's your point?"

"My point is this isn't going to be as easy as any of us want it to be. I'd love this to be simple and easy but it's not going to be. We all have to be patient with each other and not let our tempers get the better of us."

"Oh like that could happen. Too much has happened for us not to fight. Whether you like it or not she's going to take your side, she always will."

He shook his head "She's never taken my side when you and I fight. When we were kids she'd take your side because she hates seeing you upset. When we were dating and fought she'd slap me for upsetting you. She's always taken your side and she always will. I don't know what you told her but whatever you told her must have torn her in half."

"How? How could I have done that?"

"I don't know. All I know is whatever it is really is tearing her apart. She's refusing to tell me what's going on and I hate seeing you both this way."

I rolled my eyes "I highly doubt you hate seeing me upset. I really don't care what's going on with May. What does this have to do with anything? I'll tell you the answer, it has nothing to do with anything!"

"Kate-"

"Just stop! I absolutely hate your guts!"

"If you hate me so much then why would you have asked me to come?" His voice was calm, free of any anger.

"I thought you'd have helped but instead you only made this worse."

He shook his head "I didn't make this worse just by showing up. I saw the way you greeted May; you still care about her. You both say that you hate each other, you don't."

"Stop making up lies, I'm done with your lies. I'm done with a lot of things and this is just another thing I'm done with."

"I know you don't mean that."

"How?! How would you know! You don't! Stop trying to assume you know who I am! I really do hate you!"

"I'm sorry to hear that but I don't hate you; my feelings for you haven't changed. I would tell you but; it's not worth it anymore."

"I find that hard to believe. You say your feelings haven't changed but I know that's a lie, it's a bunch of bullshit."

"You wouldn't listen when I tried to explain."

"You never tried to explain! You asked me why I refused to talk to you and I told you! You never tried to explain and I really rather you didn't explain. I don't want to know why you cheated on me."

"I never cheated on you; I didn't send those messages to you. I didn't know until you stopped talking to me."

I rolled my eyes "You just can't stop lying can you?!"
"I'm not lying!"

"I'm done." I said. I turned and started to walk away.

Again he grabbed my arm, he spun me around so I was facing him. I didn't have a chance to react before his lips met mine. I pushed him away and smacked him across the face.

"WHY DID YOU DO THAT?!" I screamed.

He didn't say anything.

"Well?"

"I panicked."

"You panicked and you think that's okay?"

He shrugged "I wasn't thinking. You know I wouldn't have done that if I was thinking."

"So what if I know that. You still did it."

"I really do still care about you, I never stopped. I promise you I didn't do anything to hurt you."

"What did happen then? Why did you send those messages?"

"I didn't send them."

"Then who did?"

He ran his hand through his hair "You know the people I called my friends who were never really my friends but I hung out with them anyways?"

"How could I not? They're assholes."

"Well, they got into my phone and sent you those messages. They deleted what they sent and left what you were saying."

"How did they even get into your phone? If they deleted the messages then how did you find out what they were saying?"

"I hacked into your phone to see what upset you. I knew you wouldn't delete the messages right away. I saw them and I wanted to explain to you; you wouldn't let me."

"I didn't let you because it came from your phone. I've told you for years that those guys aren't good people, you never listened. Now you've seen the results. I hope that they're worth it."

"I've stopped talking to them."

"That doesn't change anything. You shouldn't have left your phone with them. Maybe if you hadn't then things would be different. Things happen for a reason; this is just another thing that happened for a reason. I don't care anymore. I've moved on."

He frowned; I had a feeling he could see right through my lie. "Some take longer to move on than others." he said simply.

"It's been a year."

"Doesn't matter. You want to know what happened or not?"

"Of course I want to know what happened. I also don't want to keep fighting with everyone."

"You have my word that I won't fight with May if you go back."

I looked over his shoulder to where Kelly and May stood; they were watching us. "I dunno, I feel like it'd just be weird."

"Trust me, it's already weird."

I smiled "I know you're right but still; it's gonna be weird."

"I know."

I sighed "I guess we should get back over there then."

"Yup." he turned around and started walking back. I didn't start walking right away; I was still in shock of what happened.

"Okay, look I dunno what you guys were talking about and I'm gonna pretend I didn't see what I did but how does any of this have anything to do with what you wanted to talk about?" May asked once I joined them.

I sat on the grass, they all sat once I patted the grass beside me. "It has actually a lot to do with what I want to talk to you guys about. We couldn't go a minute without yelling at each other so I think we should talk about what happened before this first."

"What got into you?" May and Kelly asked.

"Steve, what the hell did you do to her?!" May shouted.

"I didn't do anything." Steve said.

May stood up and started walking; she motioned for me to follow her. I got up and followed her. "What's up?" I asked once we were out of earshot of the others.

"'What's up?' I should be asking you that. You ran off basically crying and you come back like you want to talk about what's been going on since the beginning of the year. Kate, you've rarely done that. I've only ever seen you do that when... you've got to be freaking kidding me."

"What? What are you talking about? I've only done what when what?" I knew very well what she was talking about, I wasn't about to say anything.

"You still like him don't you. You've always liked him; you never stopped."

"That's ridiculous. You know more about me than I do; but trust me I don't like him."

She stared at me until I looked away. "HA! I knew it. Why though? He hurt you."

I stared at the grass and dug the toe of my shoe into the dirt. "Sometimes we can be wrong and jump to conclusions." I mumbled.

"That does literally nothing. Please tell me."

I sighed "He wasn't the one who said anything; it was someone else. He never sent the messages that hurt me; he didn't know until I stopped talking to him."

She was confused. "How do you know it wasn't him if you won't let him talk to you about it?"

"I let him explain; just now."

"Did you guys get back together?" she spoke slowly; as though she didn't want to know.

I shook my head "No. I know what really happened and I guess I can get over it but I'm not going to let go that easy."

"So then you're going to be hanging this over his head?"

I shrugged "Dunno, it's possible. And I wouldn't actually hang it over his head, at least not right now."

"So then what you've been doing since we've met then."

"Exactly."

"I'm sorry that I took his side. I much rather have taken your side. I just didn't know what was going on. It tore me apart knowing that you were hurting and I couldn't do anything."

"It's okay. We've always been best friends and we always will be. Best friends fight at times ya know."

She smiled "I know. It's unlike us to fight."

"I know. Life always has to test us."

"We good?"

"Always have been."

We walked back to the others and sat down. "So, you guys good?" Kelly asked as we sat down.

I nodded "Yeah. Can we talk about why I asked you guys to meet me here?"

"Well that's what we came here for. So I guess we might as well." May said.

"You already know what I know. I wasn't there so I can't really provide you with what you're looking for." Kelly said.

"I know; I still want you here. It wouldn't be the same without you." I said.

"I guess I'll start." May said. "I heard someone screaming but I didn't know who. I hid in a locker until it was over. I could hear the gunfire; I'd never been so scared. Once the gunfire stopped I stayed in the locker until someone opened it. An officer opened it and told me it was safe to come out and that I had to leave the building. I left and followed everyone else out. Everyone went to the parking lot by the football field. I found Steve and I stayed with him; until I had to go talk with an officer."

"We all had to talk with the police. Those who weren't hurt had to stay and tell them what they heard and what they saw if they saw anything." Steve said.

"I went to talk with an officer and Steve wandered off; I didn't know where he went until he came back with you. Even now I don't know why he went back to the school or why he had you. He won't tell me." May said.

I turned my head so I was looking at him; he seemed to be uncomfortable. "Why did you go back to the school? I know that you weren't supposed to." I said.

He shrugged and took a deep breath. "You really going to make me share why I went back into the school?"

"Yes." All three of us said.

"I went back in there because I refused to believe that you" he looked at me "were dead. I wouldn't believe it until I saw it with my own eyes. I didn't see anyone in the school while I was in there. No police were in there, I don't know why. I was walking down the main hall towards the big pile of rubble that was the second floor. When I got closer I saw that someone was under it and trying to get out.

"When I got there I saw that you was trying to get yourself out. I took everything off of you; it took a while but I was able to do it. The last thing I took off was a bookshelf. I wasn't able to move it to the side so I had to lift it up. Once it was off your legs you pulled yourself away. Once she was out from under it I dropped it."

"Was I able to stand?" I asked, my voice was like a whisper.

He shook his head "You wanted to but you couldn't. I didn't want to leave to get help; your skin was extremely pale once nothing was on you. I picked you up and brought you outside. I brought you over to the parking lot where you passed out. You were taken to Boston in an ambulance."

Both him and May seemed to know something they didn't want to tell me. "You were clinically dead for fifteen minutes." May said, after a while.

I stared blankly at them "How is that possible? I was dead for that amount of time and came back? That doesn't seem likely." I was shaking my head.

May placed her hands in mine. "I know but it happened. I was there; I saw you die and I saw you come back. If I hadn't seen it myself, I wouldn't have believed it."

"Still, it's hard to believe."

"I'd never lie to you, I have no plans to start. Do you really think I'd lie to you about that?"

I rolled my eyes, smiled, and laughed a little. "No; you'd never. Wait so did I like die on school grounds?"

"No, in the ambulance. They let me go; I think they would have said no in other circumstances."

"Ummmmm you looked like you'd punch them if they said no." Steve said.

She glared at him.

I laughed "I know you probably did so don't try to deny it."

"Oh alright, I would have pitched a fit if they said no."

"Where was Steve while you guys were hiding?" Kelly asked.

"I got out of the school; I was in the gym when it started so I was able to get out."

My phone buzzed and I pulled it out of my pocket. "I gotta go. I'm late." I said standing up.

"You need a ride?" May asked.

I shook my head "As much as I'd like one I rather walk home. If I cut through the woods I'd get there faster."

"The woods?" Steve asked.

I nodded "I have to, it's the fastest way home. I'm already late, besides I'm sure you guys have plans."

They all looked at me like I was crazy, they had good reason to. I'd never refuse a ride from them if I was late. Kelly looked at her watch "It's bound to be darker in the woods by now."

"Kelly's both right and wrong. It's not too dark in the woods but the ones you want to use are. We all know you can't see well in the dark." May said.

I shook my head "I know you guys are just trying to look out for me but I really do have to go. Please, just let me go alone." I was annoyed.

"What are you hiding?" Steve asked.

I rolled my eyes and shook my head. "I'm not hiding anything. Look I'll call you guys later, I really have to go." I quickly turned away and ran towards the bridge.

I slowed down to a walk once I was in the woods. Ever since the old abandoned building closed down the trees took over again. I don't know why the place was closed or why it's still standing even though the parking lot was torn up. It's rumored that a group of people tore up the parking lot and planted a whole bunch of trees, no one has ever been able to figure out if it's true or not.

The building was caving in on all sides and leaning heavily to one side. The sun was blocked by the branches above, making the small plants below hard to see. These woods never had a path and no one's ever cared to make one. I guess it's because these woods are actually extremely dangerous once the ground became difficult to see.

The flashlight on my phone doesn't work so I had no source of light. I'd never been in these woods when you couldn't see, let alone much during the day. I only knew this being the fastest way home because well I'd spend a lot of time in here after school these past few months.

"Kate, wait up." Steve said.

I took a deep breath and willed myself to not say anything.

Stepping into stride beside me he spoke "You know these woods aren't a good place to be now."

I rolled my eyes "I'm well aware of that. Does May know you're here?"

"She knows. She's going to your house. I'm walking with you so that you're not alone in here."

"Whatever. Just please don't try to see my parents, if they're outside you don't show your face, you hide. If they're inside you don't follow me."

"Do you hear that?" he whispered.

I shook my head "No." I heard something moving around nearby and assumed it was the wind.

"SHIT!" Steve shouted.

I looked to the side, he wasn't there. I looked behind me and saw that he was curled in a ball, he was getting the crap beat out of him.

I took out my phone and snapped a photo. I was trying to be silent but my ringer was on resulting in my phone making a noise I as I took the image, the flash went off as well.

Whoever it was looked at me and smirked. I screamed, turned around and ran. The plants and bushes brushed against my arms and legs as I ran. I ran straight through, I didn't take the turn I had to to get home. I reached the point where I could see the street, I ran towards the street. The guy chasing me stayed about fifty feet into the woods.

I stood on the side of the road and took another picture of him hiding in the woods. He flipped me off but didn't move. I sighed and started down the road.

A moment later a car pulled over not far in front of me; the drivers door opened and May poked her head out. "Hey, what happened?"

I shook my head.

"Where's Steve?"

I shrugged "Dunno."

"Get in." May demanded.

I got into her car through the backseat; I crawled up front and put on the seat belt. I leaned my head against the window.

"What happened? Please tell me he's okay."

"I wish I could." I mumbled "Can we go to the police station?"

She sighed; I knew she was worried. "Okay. You're lucky that your parents don't need to be there."

I snorted "Maybe my parents don't need to be there but you're not eighteen yet so you're parents have to be there. Even if you were eighteen your parents would still end up there."

"What? Why?" her voice filled with fear.

I sighed and shook my head "He shouldn't have gone. I knew I should have sent him back." I said more to myself than to May.

"Kate, what happened to him?" her voice cracked.

I sighed "I don't really know."

She turned in to the parking lot and parked the car. We both got out and went inside. I took several deep breaths; I didn't want to have a panic attack, I knew it'd come anyways.

"Can I help you?" someone at the window asked.

Fear flooded my voice as I spoke. "Yeah,. I need to report something. It's urgent."

"I'll find someone for you to talk with."

May's mom came out of the door, she smiled at the sight of her daughter. Her smile quickly faded and changed to worry a moment later.

"What's wrong? Is everything okay? Are you girls in trouble?"

I looked at May, I turned back to her mother and sighed. "You're not going to like this and you won't be thrilled."

"What happened?"

"Well I was walking home; I was late so I figured I'd cut through the woods since it's faster. Steve and May both offered me a ride home, I refused. I took off running so they wouldn't keep asking me, well Steve went after me. He caught up with me not long after I got into the woods. He swore, loudly and when I turned around to see why he had swore, he was getting the crap beat out of him." I pulled out my phone and showed her the two images.

Her face went pale "My baby." she mumbled. She stood frozen on the spot.

May approached her mother slowly "Mom?"

Her mother shook her head and didn't say anything.

Another officer came out, I quickly recognized him as her partner, Justin. "Wilma you okay?"

Again she shook her head.

"What's up with her?" he asked.

"Steve, woods, hurt." Wilma said before bolting out the door.

Justin ran after her, May and I exchanged a worried look before running after them. Justin was getting into the car as Wilma was starting the car, the door wasn't even closed before she started driving.

May and I jumped into her car and drove away. By the time we got back to the edge of the woods Justin was standing against the car and speaking into the radio.

May and I walked over to him, unsure of what to do. He saw us and motioned for us to come closer. "Before you ask, I don't know where she went. She pulled the car onto to curb and got out. She took off running and wouldn't come back when I called her back."

"Is she gonna lose her job?" May asked.

Justin shook his head "I don't think so. She's good at what she does. She was the only one available to come talk to you guys at the time. You know that we're not supposed to do anything involving our families. I don't think it's likely that she'll lose her job, she's definitely going to get in trouble."

"Okay." May mumbled.

I put my arm around her, I knew she was scared. She gave me a small smile and put her arm around me.

"Hey, we'll find him. I promise." Justin said.

I didn't say anything, I knew I had to keep my mouth shut. Tomorrow is May and Steve's birthday, they've always been together for their birthday. Never once have they spent the day apart, this may be the first year they aren't together. Steve means a lot to her, their birthday means a lot to her.

Another police car pulled up onto the curb, he walked towards us. I knew full on that May and I aren't supposed to be near Justin since he's on scene. We walked away hoping that Justin wouldn't get in trouble.

A gray chevy pulled over on the side of the road. Mays father stepped out of the car and came over to us. He wrapped his arms around May and held onto her, he kissed the top of her head. "You okay?" He asked.

"I wasn't there. Kate was."

He looked over at me; I couldn't read his expression. "What were the two of you doing in the woods?"

"I was trying to get home, I was late and cutting through those woods is the fastest way home. I didn't ask him to follow me, he followed me himself."

He sighed "Where's your mother?"

"She ran into the woods." May said.

"Did Justin try to stop her?"

We both nodded "She wouldn't listen. He doesn't know where she went; he didn't go after her. Neither of them are really supposed to have anything to do with this, more so Mom."

He sighed "Kate, how deep were you in those woods? Where were you in those woods? There's no path." He was trying to keep his voice steady and free of any emotion.

"I don't honestly know. I mean I could show you where we were, but I couldn't tell you how deep in we were. I don't think we were that deep though."

Mays father was staring at the trees; he shook his head after a while. I turned to see why he was shaking his head; Wilma had her arms pinned to her sides, she was being escorted out of the woods.

She jerked herself free, instead of going back into the woods she came over to where we stood. "My baby." she said softly.

"He'll be okay."

"Steve, my son is missing! The last time he was seen he was getting beat up! How do you think he's going to be okay!" Wilma shouted.

I always forget that Steve is named after his father. It's rare for Wilma to refer to her husband as Steve. Normally Wilma, and everyone else refers to him by his middle name; Peter.

May pulled into my driveway and I got out. "Thanks for the ride. You still want me to come over tomorrow?"

She shrugged "Might as well. Mom and Dad probably won't mind. I don't think they'd really want you to stay away."

"Well I'm here if you need me. Just a phone call away."

She gave me a small smile; I stepped onto the front lawn as she drove down the driveway and down the street. I sighed and walked up the front steps.

I walked inside and went into my fathers den. He was sitting at his desk reading something on the computer.

"Hey." I said as I sat on the small couch.

He looked up over the screen; he seemed to be studying her expression. "How'd you get all those cuts?"

"Oh I cut through the woods since I was running late."

He looked at the clock "You're more than a little late. Did you get lost in the woods?"

I shook my head "No. I know the way to get from the park-"

He glared at me "Which park?" he was struggling to keep any strain from his voice.

"The one over by the school."

"An elementary school? The high school?"

"The high school, we live too far away from the elementary schools."

He shook his head and rubbed the side of his face. "Let me get this straight. You know we don't want you in those woods, and you knew the way you needed to go to get home. This wasn't your first time in those woods was it?"

"Well no, I've been there a lot. Mostly after school so I've never been in there when it's dark or close to dark. This is the first time."

"Does Mom know?"

I shook my head "I never thought to tell her."

He leaned back in his chair and sighed. "Did she ever ask why you have small cuts all over you?"

Again I shook my head "No. I've never gotten small cuts before."

"Why'd you get cut this time?"

I wanted to lie; I knew that lying wouldn't be any good. They'd find out at some point, I'd be better off telling him. I took a deep breath and told him about what happened.

When I finished he was silent for awhile. "So Steve went after you so you wouldn't be alone and ended up getting beat up by someone that you don't know."

I nodded. "I got a picture but the flash went off and my phone made the camera clicking noise. He saw me so I ran; he ran after me. He wouldn't go any further than being like fifty feet into the woods. It was like he couldn't leave the woods without something happening to him."

Dad didn't say anything; he was quickly typing something on his computer. A few minutes passed before he called me over to him; I stood behind him. "Does this look familiar?"

On the screen was an image of three ghostly pale people; they appeared to be human but didn't come across as a full on person. They weren't smiling nor were they looking at the camera; they didn't seem to even know the picture was taken. Their clothes were rags and didn't even look like clothes. Their hair stuck out odd angles; it was bright purple.

I pulled out my phone and looked at the images; the only difference was that the guy on my phone had bright silver hair and seemed to extremely young to have silver hair.

"Yeah, they look familiar but they have purple hair, this one has silver hair."

I showed him the image I took once I was out of the woods. He mumbled to himself; I couldn't hear too well. It sounded as though he said "He's one of them." I wasn't positive nor was I going to ask.

"Kate, please go find Mom and tell her I need to speak with her. I also don't want you to be in here after you find Mom; you don't need to about this."

I shrugged and went to the kitchen, Mom wasn't there. I went upstairs and found her hanging something on the wall. "Hey Mom."

She didn't look at me; she was focusing on what she was doing. "What's up? You missed supper; there's some leftovers in the fridge if you want them."

"Oh ok; sorry I missed supper by the way."

"That's okay; just don't do it again. Do you need anything else?"

"Uh yeah. Dad's in his den; he wants to talk with you."

"Oh okay. Could you go tell him I'll be right there?"

"Sure."

I went back downstairs and into my father's den. "Mom said she'll be right down."

"Ok, thanks."

I went back to the kitchen; I wanted to get some of the leftovers from the fridge, instead I went down to the basement. I flicked on the lights and wandered around.

I went to the back corner of the basement; none of us ever end up in this corner. The corner consisted of many things that my parents no longer used nor could bring themselves to get rid of.

Wedged in the corner was a small pile of boxes; not much dust could be seen. The boxes around had dust that was visible; even in the dark.. The small pile of boxes in front of me had so little dust that it could only be seen when you put your fingers on the box.

"Why isn't there much dust?" I wondered aloud.

"Kate?" Dad called down the stairs.

"I'm down here." I shouted over my shoulder.

I could hear him walking down the stairs. "Where?"

"In the back corner."

"Why are you back here?"

"I dunno."

"Are you looking for a place to have a party?" Dad teased.

"No."

"Looking for a place to hide tomorrow so you don't have to go back to school?"

"No. As much as I don't want to go back to school; I'm not looking for a place to hide. Besides I'm all caught up."

He looked at me "If you're all caught up then I'd say it's safe to say that you'll be just fine tomorrow. I'm proud of you by the way."

"For what? I haven't done anything recently that you should be proud of."

He smiled and put his hand on my shoulder. "You've done a lot that I should be proud of you for. I'd be a horrible father if I wasn't proud of you. Proud of you for having the courage to face everyone at school, and proud of how far you've come these past few months."

I smiled "Thanks Dad."

"Why don't we go back upstairs, Mom and I want to talk with you." There was a tone in his voice that concerned me; why I wasn't sure, I knew I'd soon find out.

I followed Dad into the living room, he sat on the couch, Mom sat beside him, and I sat in the oversized chair.

"Kate, as you know your father had been away for a while. Do you remember why he went away?" Mom spoke slowly.

"I know he was gone for awhile and I know why. I didn't lose that much of my memory."

"Please don't be sarcastic." Dad said.

"Sorry."

Mom sighed "Dad's been talking with his publishers-"

"HE CAN'T GO BACK!' I shouted.

"He's not going anywhere." Mom said quickly. "As I was saying, he's been talking with his publishers, they've caved and are allowing him to be here with us, he won't have to go back to California for a while. Every once in a while he will need to go back, they're gonna try to work around his schedule so he can be here with us. Now that all of that is worked out, they're gonna be working on figuring out who did tell everyone that he had been writing those books; Dad's gonna be working on that as well, he'll be here."

"Really? He's able to stay? He doesn't have to go back?!"

Dad shook his head "Not for awhile."

I got up and hugged both my parents. "Kate, could you please go sit back down, there's something else we need to talk to you about." Mom said.

I sighed and went back to the chair. "What's up? Am I finally getting a younger sibling?"

Both my parents shook their heads "Not today." Mom said.

I frowned.

"Do you remember the story I used to tell you when you were little?" Dad asked.

I nodded "It was of this creature that lived in the woods and feasted on anyone who passed through their woods once it got dark If there was a group, they'd try to get everyone, they almost always succeed. If they step into the open, they die within twenty four hours. Even if they really want something, they won't step out into the open to get it."

Dad nodded "Do you remember what I told you they looked like?"

I shook my head.

"They have extremely pale skin, brightly colored hair, their natural hair colors aren't the typical ones, theirs tend to be, blue, silver, and purple."

"What does this have anything to do with me?" Once I spoke, I knew what the answer was. I put my head into hands. "You've gotta be kidding me!" I moaned.

"Kate, we want you to know how lucky you are that you got away." Mom said.

"As for Steve, personally I think he got what he deserved." Dad said.

I looked up and glared at him. "How could you say something like that!" I screamed.

"He hurt my baby! I have no respect for anyone who hurts my baby." Dad said.

I took several deep breaths before speaking. "It wasn't his fault, he didn't send the messages."

"I'm sorry, did you say massages?!"

I nodded "I never told you?"

"No." Both my parents said.

I felt my face turn red. "My bad. That's not my point though. My point is, he didn't know it happened."

"You said he knew." Dad protested.

I nodded "I know, he hacked into my phone to see why I was upset."

Dad rolled his eyes, I knew he wasn't buying into this. "Kate, I know how much he meant to you, you can't lie to yourself over what really happened."

"I'M NOT LYING! I'M TELLING YOU THE TRUTH! I shouted.

"Be reasonable! Listen to yourself!"

I rolled my eyes "YOU'RE THE ONE WHO NEEDS TO BE REASONABLE! YOU WON'T BELIEVE ME WHEN I'M TELLING YOU THE TRUTH!" I sprang to my feet, ran up the stairs, went to my room, slammed the door behind me and crawled into bed.

The next morning, I got ready in silence. Neither of my parents were up, as it was not the time I normally get up for school. I hid my school bag in the basement, packed a small bag with a bottle of water, my phone and a few dollars. I wrote a note and hid it under my keyboard, they'd see it; the corner was sticking out. Hopefully they wouldn't see it right away. I wrote another note and pinned it to the fridge. The one I pinned to the fridge would make it so they wouldn't worry until the school day was over.

I opened the door and started down the street. The sun was just starting to rise, if I hurried I might be able to have them find me. I hoped that I'd be able to find where they are first.

As I approached the woods, I looked around to see if anyone was around, as predicted no one was around. I walked through the woods looking for the old abandoned building, I couldn't find it. All day long I walked through the woods searching. There was no sign of the building.

As the sun began to set and it became harder to see in the woods, I heard a noise. It sounded as though someone was whistling, I looked around, I couldn't see anyone. Right in front of me, the old abandoned building appeared, I crept closer, hoping no one would see me.

I crept around all sides of the building, nobody was too be seen. I peered through the last window on the main floor, I saw a staircase leading up to the second floor. I crawled through the window and landed silently at the base of the stairs. I walked up the stairs, careful not to make a sound.

In any of the doorways, there was no door. I peered into each one, each room was empty. Through the door at the very end of the hall, was another staircase, this one went up, the only problem was there was no third floor, not even access to the roof. Curious, I went up the stairs, as if by magic there was a third floor. I could hear people moving around, I stuck to the shadows. I crept along the back wall, careful not to make a sound.

As I moved along the wall, I fell backwards, somehow they didn't hear me fall. Slowly I got to my feet, I saw Steve sitting against the wall, he was looking at me. He put his finger to his lips, I nodded. Slowly I approached him, he leaned forward exposing a rope, his hands were tied to the wall. Quickly I untied the rope, the second the rope hit the wall, a loud screeching noise begin.

Frozen in fear we watched the door, maybe ten human like creatures appeared, all with pale skin, and brightly colored hair. All of them had looks that could kill. "You brat!" they all shouted.

I stood frozen, unable to move. I was lifted off my feet and thrown out the window. I landed hard on the ground, I looked up and saw Steve was falling out the first floor window. I got to my feet just as he grabbed my hand, we were running. We ran through the woods as fast as we coud. Neither of us said a word until we reached an open field.

Panting and out of breath, we sat down. "Why didn't you jump from the third floor?" I asked, catching my breath.

"We were on the first floor, I don't understand it, The stairs you used took you back to the first floor but changed it to what you saw. Please tell me you aren't alone."

I started pulling at the grass, a sign that I was in fact alone.

"Damnit, Kate. Why?"

I closed my eyes and sighed. "My parents hate you." I said.

"What?"

"I said-"

"I know what you said, why do they hate me."

"They think that you sent those messages. I tried to tell them that it wasn't you, they didn't believe me."

"Okay… but what does that have to do with why you're here alone?"

"Do you really think I'd have come alone if they believed me?"

"Kate, I don't see why your parents not believing you has anything to do with why you came."

I sighed "I thought that if you told them, they'd believe it."

"I doubt that's why. Please tell me the truth, you know you can tell me anything."

"Okay, well you have to promise not to think I'm insane."

"Okay?"

I told him what my parents had told me the night before, when I finished he was confused.

"Let me get this straight, those, whatever they are, can't be in the open because they die within twenty four hours, they feed off of people who are in the woods at night, and your Dad used this as a bedtime story when you were little?"

I nodded "Pretty much. I don't think he believed they were real until last night." I closed my eyes "He's gonna kill me when they find me."

Steve grabbed my hand and squeezed it. "He's not gonna kill you, I won't let him."

I smiled "By the way happy birthday."

"Thanks, it'd be better if we were back home and not in the middle of nowhere. Did you wish May a happy birthday?"

I shook my head "I didn't text her and I didn't go to school."

His eyes grew wide "You skipped school?"

I nodded.

"Okay, well now your parents are gonna kill you."

I slapped him; he laughed. "I knew you'd do that.

I smiled. "I missed being with you." I confessed.

"Same here."

"What are we?" I mumbled.

"I'm not sure."

"What do you want us to be?" I asked.

"You know the answer to that, I dunno if it's mutual though."

I was silent, I wanted to be with him again, I wanted him to be mine; at the same time, I knew it wouldn't be the same. I closed my eyes "Will things ever be the same?"

He put his hand on my cheek, I felt his lips on mine, a moment later he pulled away; his forehead against mine. "Things will never be the same, nothing will be the same." he whispered, his hand still on my cheek.

My heart was pounding, I was fighting the urge to kiss him, in the end, my heart won. I wrapped my arms around his neck, and kissed him. He wrapped his arms around my waist, holding me tight.

A few seconds later I pulled away, I put my head against his shoulder. "Do you know where we are?" I asked.

He looked around "I was hoping you did."

***

I grabbed his arm, we were lost, out in the middle of nowhere, alone, at night. I wanted nothing more to be back at home, or at least to know where I was. I reached into my bag and pulled out my phone, no signal. "We're stuck, I have no signal, I can't find out where we are."

"Look to see if there's any public wifi around you can use. If there is, we can look up where we are and figure out if we need to call for a ride or not."

"Nothing's showing up. Do you think we should walk around to see if we can find anyone?"

"It's getting dark and considering we're in the middle of a field, I'd say that's a wise choice."

We both stood up and started walking; at some point we ended up holding hands. We must have been walking for a couple hours before we even saw a faint trace of light, it took us another hour to even reach the source of the light.

It came from a large stadium, across the street from the stadium was a small police station. I streed us towards the station. "Can I help you?" someone said as we walked in.

"Could you tell us where we are?" Steve said.

"Why, you're in Littleton."

"Mass?"

She shook her head "Nope, Maine."

My mouth fell open "You mean we are almost six hours away from home?"

"Where is your home?"

"We live in Massachusetts."

"Well then it's very possible that you're six hours away. How old are you two?"

"We're eighteen."

"Are you still in high school?"

I nodded.

"Do your parents know you're here?"

I shook my head.

"Would like to explain why?"

I nodded. "We were in the woods in town, and when we came out, we were in a big open field. We walked around for hours before we came to any civilization."

"You kids high?"

I shook my head "No ma'am I'm telling you the truth."

"Do you know you're parents numbers?"

"Yes ma'am."

She motioned for us to follow her, we followed her to a small office. "Could one of you please type in the number you want me to use."

Steve typed in a number and we sat in silence.

"Hello, this is Detective Hudson of the Littleton Police."

"No ma'am in Maine."

Through the phone we heard Wilma shout "IN MAINE!"

"Yes ma'am, in Maine."

She covered the bottom part of the phone, what are your names?"
"I'm Kate."

"I'm Steve."

"Kate and Steve?" she said into the phone.

"Yes ma'am they're both here."

"I'm too sure, they told me a very weird story, I'm not sure if I believe them. Have you known either of them to ever be high?"

"I'm asking because, well usually only people who are high have that crazy of stories."

"Kate's parents are with you?"

"Oh good."

"Okay, see you soon." she put the phone back on the receiver and looked at us. "Your parents will be here as soon as they can. Follow me please." She stood up and walked to the door, we followed.

She lead us to a rom, I guess a room where people had to wait for their rides, as there was a glass window that allowed you to see into the entrance way.

"Please stay here until your parents get here. Feel free to take some water." She pointed over to a bubbler and a stack of cups. "The door's always unlocked but we ask that you stay here, there's a bathroom through that door there." She pointed to a door on the back wall before leaving and closing the door behind her.

We sat down, we were facing the door, we wouldn't be able to see when our parents got here. I laced my fingers through Steves and put my head on his shoulder. I took out my phone to check the time, midnight, my phone powered off, the battery was dead.

I opened my eyes, Steve's head was on top of mine, I looked at the clock on the wall, quarter of six, I closed my eyes.

I must have dozed off again, when I awoke it was ten past six, the sun was shining through the windows, Steve was still asleep. The door opened, Detective Hudson had opened the door. I jabbed my finger against his ribcage as our parents and May appeared in the doorway. "I'm awake." Steve shouted, his face quickly turned red.

I stood up and went over to my parents, Dad put his arms around me and held me tight. "I know you were telling the truth, that doesn't excuse you from skipping school yesterday or anything. I hope you know how much trouble you're in."

"I know Dad, I know."

I hugged Mom next, her face was bright red, even she held me tight. "You were so stupid. Never do that again. You're in so much trouble. I'm so happy you're safe."

"I'm sorry."

"I know."

After Mom let me go, I stood in front of them, avoiding their glares. May came over and hugged me. "Do I want to know why you were like that?"

"Probably."

"You gonna tell me?"

"Not right now."

"You know, you're the only one who's in major trouble."

"No kidding."

"I'm glad you're both okay."

"Me too."

"Why did you do it?"

"I'll tell you later."

"Ok. Do I want to know what happened?"

"Parts of it."

"I love you, but I hate you."

"I know."

"You're like my sister, I get away with it."

"I know."

"Thank you for finding him."

"You're welcome."

Once again I was standing in front of my parents, I knew there was no way they'd let me go anywhere with Steve again; I detested the thought. Dad put his hand on my shoulder and steered me out to the car. I got in the back seat and leaned my head against the window.

Once on the highway, Dad broke the silence, Mom was driving. "Kate, what were you thinking?"

"I was thinking that I was gonna save my friend."

Dad scoffed "I don't think someone who hurt you can be considered a friend. And I don't appreciate the way you were sitting."

"We were sleeping in effing chairs!" I protested.

"Do you think I care? Kate, I may be 'old' but I am your father. I don't approve of him."

"DAD! I told you the truth! He didn't do that! It wasn't his fault! Why don't you believe me!"

"Because! I know how that kind of thing works! He's gonna play dumb to get back together with you so he can hurt you worse!"

"MOM!"

"Shaun, you know that by telling her she can't be around him will only make her want to be with him more."

"So? I don't want my baby girl to get hurt!"

"Dad-"

"You stay out of this. Until you start acting like an adult, you'll be treated like a child."

"SHAUN! You know she isn't a child! You've always trusted her! Why don't you trust her anymore?! What changed that trust you had in her? Last night you were so confident that she knew what she was doing! You went to the basement and when you came back, you said you'd kill her if she was found!"

"DAD!" I shouted.

"KATE STAY OUT!" he shouted. "I don't trust her! Not anymore!"

"WHY DON'T YOU TRUST ME?! WHAT DID I DO?!"

"KATE BUD OUT!"

I'd only ever seen him this angry once, it was with his brother, I was too little to understand and I no longer remember what they were fighting about. All I can remember was that after that, they didn't talk for three years. I didn't want him to be mad at me, yet I knew not of why he was angry.

"Shaun, what is wrong with you?! You adore her! Why are you so angry all of a sudden?!"

"Me angry? Nah, I'm beyond angry, I'm flat out hurt."

Mom slammed on the breaks, Dad never admitted to being hurt before, it wasn't like him. Mom quickly got the car moving again. "Why are you hurt?" Mom asked.

"Ask your daughter." Dad said, annoyed.

"Kate-"

I shrugged "I dunno what he's talking about."

Dad huffed "Your necklace, I found it in the basement in the bottom of a box."

"What?"

"Why did you put the necklace in that box?"

"I don't remember putting it in any box. I thought I lost it."

"I get you'd be mad at me for leaving, but that doesn't mean you had to take my picture out of the locket."

"I didn't take your picture out."

"You say you didn't take my picture out when you did. Kate, I opened the locket, I know you took my picture out of there."

I shook my head "I'd never take your picture out of there. Dad, I know better. I added a picture to it, I never took yours out."

He huffed "The person you added, you might as well have just taken me out of it completely."

I sighed "Dad-"

"Just forget. I took the liberty of removing him, I burned the picture."

My heart sank, I couldn't believe what my father was telling me. I didn't say anything, he knew he hurt me and he didn't care.

"Shaun, she's growing up, she's going to find someone, that doesn't mean she's not going to stop needing you. She's always told you that she's gonna need you." Mom said.

Dad huffed. "If she still needs me then why does she bother with boys?"

Mom shook her head. "You're just like your father, you swore you were never going to be like him and yet here you are."

The one thing Dad hates is being compared to his father. His father was extremely protective of his sisters, Dad hated watching it. He promised me he'd never do that to me, yet he is.

"I'm nothing like him." Dad spat.

I leaned my head against the window, I wanted nothing more than for all of this to go away.

Mom sighed "I know you aren't, that doesn't change that your acting like him. Shaun, she's going to make her own mistakes, we both know that we can't baby her anymore, all we can do is be there for her when she needs us."

"So you agree that she's making a mistake in choosing to give him another chance?"

"I never said that."

"Then you want her to give him another chance?"

"I never said that either."

"Then what are you saying?!"

"I'm saying let her decide on her own. Since it looks like she's chosen to forgive him, that's her choice. I'd like to know why, but it's her choice on whether or not she tells us. Shaun, I get that she's your little girl, she's my little girl as well, she's eighteen, she has to make her own choices."

"Do you agree with her choices?"

"I'm choosing to trust my daughter. I trust that she thinks she's making the right choice. I'm going to support my daughter in whatever she chooses."

"What happened to telling her what she could and couldn't do her whole life?"

I knew what Dad was talking about, before I was born my parents had said they'd try to influence my choices in life, no matter how old I was. Of course that's not what happened, Mom says it's because I ended up being a good kid. Dad on the other hand, I know he wants me to be independent, while at the same time he wants me to always want him around. Dad's always struggled with me growing up and not needing him as much.

Mom sighed "Shaun, you know she's not stupid. I know you trust her. I know you don't want her to get hurt, I don't want her to get hurt either, she has to learn for herself."

"I don't want her to get hurt, you're right about that. I also want her to not have to find out for herself, I want her to listen to why she should listen."

"He's her best friends brother, you wouldn't keep her away from her best friend, I know you wouldn't. Shaun,"

"Jenna, I'm not going to keep her away from her best friend, I wouldn't do that. I want to keep her away from Steve, I don't care how hard it is, I'm going to do it."

"Dad, please, please believe me. I wouldn't lie to you."

"I told you, I don't want you to be around him. Whether you're friends with him or whatever, I don't want you around him."

"Daddy-"

He huffed, I stopped talking. "Kate, I'm going to give you one more chance, I want you to be honest with me. Why do you want to be around him again?"

"I told you, he didn't send the messages, someone else did. He didn't know it happened until after I got mad at him."

"If he didn't send the messages or know about it, how did he find out?"

"He found out because he went into my phone and saw them."

"Why did he go into your phone?"

"I had left it on a table while I was hanging out with May at their house."

"Didn't you have a password?"

"Yeah, he knew it at the time, I hadn't changed it when he looked."

"Does he know who sent the messages?"

"Yeah."

"Who?"

"You know how there were these kids that he was trying to become friends with?"

"I remember the assholes."

"They sent them."

"Does he have proof that they sent them?"

I thought for a moment, I never asked him how he was so sure it was them. "I'm not completely sure, to be honest. I could ask him."

"How would he have proof?"

"If they were at his house, they have cameras, if not then I dunno."

"So you don't know if he has any proof that they sent them?"

"No."

"Ask him."

"What?"
"You heard me, ask him."

I didn't say anything.

"Well, call him or text him and ask him."

"He doesn't have his phone, it was left in his car, at the park."

"Then ask May to ask him."

"Okay."

I quickly typed out a message to May, she responded in a matter of seconds. "She can't answer me right now. She says she'll get back to me when she can and that she'll ask him."

Dad grunted in response.

When the three of us got home, it was determined that I'd be grounded for three weeks, I'd have no access to any technology unless it was for school work.

After three weeks, I got my phone and computer back. I'd been cleared by the doctor to drive again, that happened a few days after I had gotten home, from Maine that is. Even though I was able to drive, I didn't drive much. I'd been walking more. I quickly learned that the more physical activity I did during the day, the less likely it'd be that I'd end up hurting myself.

Doctors were still having a hard time figuring out what exactly happened to my back, all they're asking me to do is to do whatever I can to keep it so my back doesn't have a chance to get wore. Which means I do a lot more physical activity during the day, even just doing a lot of walking helps. On the days that it's cold and rainy, those are the worst, I just push through the pain and do what I have to do. I refuse to let any amount of pain stop me, within reason that is.

I sat in the middle of the football field, it was a hot and humid day, classes were still going on and had to be completed. The amount of damage that had been done to the school was so bad that the town had to build small structures for classes to be held in. There was no electricity in any of them, meaning no heat and no fans. The effects have been felt throughout the whole town, everyone hates it.

The amount of annoyance it caused to most of the town resulted in a lot of people from the town donating supplies and money to rebuild the school. Without everyone from town helping, the school wouldn't have been able to hold classes, the high schoolers would have been sent to different surrounding schools. With the donations from everyone, the town was able to put up the structures that allowed for classes to be held, and keep everyone dry.

What did everyone do for a bathroom? They kept electricity in the clubhouse on as long as they could. They had to shut it off a few days ago. Now that the whole school property doesn't have power, the small business that recently opened across the street has been allowing students and faculty to use their restrooms.

There's only a few days of school left for the seniors, we get out the last day of May this year, everyone else at the high school gets out at the end of June. They had to add time on for the seniors because even after winter break was over, they weren't ready. The elementary and middle schools get out on time, just the high school that is delayed, the State approved it and the whole town understands why it's being done.

I was squinting, trying to read the directions on the paper in front of me. "Can either of you read what's on the paper?"

"If you had your glasses, you'd be able to read it." Kelly said.

"No kidding. Alas, I was in a rush this morning."

"Rough night?" May asked.

"I couldn't do anything. It was terrible."

"Maybe if you had died like you were supposed to, you'd not be in any pain."

I froze, I didn't recognize the voice, at least I thought I didn't.

"Kate, you okay?" May and Kelly asked.

"I dunno. Did you guys hear something?"

"You're hearing things? Are you insane?"

May slapped Kelly's shoulder. "You shouldn't say that. Kate what did you hear?"

"A voice, I dunno where it came from, I don't know if I've even heard it before."

"The same thing's been happening to me." Steve said, sitting down, joining us.

"You've been hearing things?" all three of us asked.

He nodded "I've been hearing things for a while, I've just kept my mouth shut."

"Why would you keep your mouth shut? It could be dangerous!" May shouted.

Steve shrugged "Until recently, I didn't have a reason to be worried."

"What the hell does that mean?" the three of us asked.

Again, he shrugged. "Honestly, I have no idea what it means myself."

"What do you mean by you didn't have a reason to be worried until recently?" I asked.

"I don't think I should be telling you here."

"There's no secrets between the four of us." I said.

Steve rolled his eyes.

"Why'd you roll your eyes? What are you hiding?" May asked.

"I'd like to know the same." Kelly said.

"Same here." I said.

"You lie. Kelly and I both know that you two have been hiding something."

"You know what happened, I told you that."

She shook her head "That's not what I mean and you know it. You still haven't told me about what happened and how you ended up in Maine."

"I did tell you!" Steve shouted.

"Not you! Kate hasn't told me anything."

"I was grounded!"

"You still could have told me while we were at school."

"What? Tell you what you already know?"

"I asked you if I wanted to know something, on why you were the way you were, you'd said you'd tell me, you have yet to tell me."

"How can I give you an answer to something I don't understand myself?"

"What's there to understand?!"

We both jumped to our feet, we were both pulled back down.

"May, if she doesn't have an answer for you, you can't expect her to tell you one." Kelly said.

"She could at least tell me what happened!"

"NOTHING HAPPENED!" I shouted.

"Is there a problem over here?" Mrs. Z asked.

All four of us started talking at once. Mrs. Z held up her hand and we all stopped talking. "I can't understand you all when you're all talking at once. Now one at a time, please tell me what the problem is. To prevent any further issues, I will choose who speaks, and when. Kelly you may start."

"Long story short, Kate was complaining that she couldn't read what's on her paper, May's upset because she thinks that Kate and Steve are hiding something from her and I got lost after that."

"Steve, you next."

"I joined later, I don't know what they were talking about before, I had said I wasn't worried about something, they all think I should be worried and somehow we got to May and Kate fighting over what Kate knows."

"May, your turn."

"Like, Kelly said, Kate had been complaining about not being able to see what's on her paper. She froze, like something startled her. She said she heard something, Steve joined and said he'd been hearing things as well, but he isn't worried about it. We all told him that he should be worried about. Kate had said she'd tell me something I'd want to know, but she hasn't told me what it is and I'd like to know what the heck she's not telling me."

"Kate, what do you have to say?"

"Same as May, Kelly, and Steve, there's no point in repeating what they've already said."

"First of all, I want you to watch that tone of yours, I know it's hard for you, but you need to. Second of all, in the last four years, I've seen you all fight and get along very well. I've never seen any of you fight like you just were. I'm aware that friends fight, and all that, however I don't think this is that."

"What do you think it is?"

"If you haven't figured out the answer, then it must not yet be clear. In time it'll become clear. I could tell you, however that'll take away part of the lesson there is to be learned from all of this. Now, going back to this problem, May, if she hasn't given you an answer, she may not have one to give you. I'm sure she'd give you one if she had one to give you."

May opened her mouth to protest but thought better of it.

"Mrs. Z, what do you mean? What lesson?" Steve asked.

She sighed "It's a lesson that doesn't come out of a book, it's a lesson that can't be taught in a classroom or anywhere. It's one that not everyone learns first hand; everyone says they understand it, when in reality they really may not."

"Mrs. Z, did you learn this lesson already?" Kelly asked.

She nodded "I wish I hadn't had to learn it first hand. Maybe if I hadn't done what I did, I'd be somewhere else."

"Does it have something to do with the drive that you gave me?" I asked

She nodded, turned and walked away.

"What drive? What is even a drive?" Kelly asked.

"A flash drive, she gave me a flash drive back in the beginning of the year."

"Did you look at it?" May asked.

I shook my head "I mean, I put it into my computer, but I never really went through it."

"Is it still on your computer?" Steve asked.

Again, I shook my head "No, I never copied them to the desktop. It's still only on the drive. And I lost it."

"Why did you lose it?" May asked.

"I didn't try to, I threw it into a drawer and forgot about it. I don't even remember which drawer I put it in."

"Maybe if you hadn't done that-" Steve slapped her arm. "What that hell was that for?" May shouted.

"You can be nice, how was she supposed to know it held something Mrs. Z wanted her to know if she hasn't looked through it." Steve said.

"I knew it had something she wanted me to know, she told me it did. I thought it had something that she thought would remind me of myself. I guess not."

"Wait, if you haven't gone through it, then how did you figure out that's what she meant so fast?" Kelly asked.

I shrugged "Beats me. She's known me for years though, I don't know why or how, I just know know she has."

"She's known you for years? Like how long?" May asked.

"Like preschool, maybe longer."

"I wouldn't go through it, at least not right now. If she has known you since preschool, then she would have told you in person. She wouldn't have given you a flash drive." Steve said.

"Why?" Kelly, May and I asked.

"May, you know what Mom's been saying, they haven't found anyone to blame on the destruction of the school."

"She's also told us not to do anything about it or talk about it."

"Wait, they haven't found anyone?" I asked.

Steve and May both shook their heads. "The cameras that were in the school, they ended up being on a loop, no one knows how they got in the school. All the cameras have the same loop and since they aren't checked often, no one realized it until they went to get the footage." May said.

"That doesn't make any sense, who could have possible wanted a school to be destroyed that bad?" Kelly asked.

"That's what everyone's trying to figure out. No one knows why it happened, there was a lot of things they had to bypass to have been able to even get on school grounds with those kinds of things."

My mind was racing, everything from the past year that I hadn't understood floated in and out of my thoughts, until finally everything fell into place. No sooner has it clicked was my face was in my hands. "You've gotta be kidding me! Why didn't I see it sooner?!"

"Kate, you okay?"

"I gotta talk with my dad, now." I said. I stood up and too off running. I ran home, I didn't slow down until I was inside.

"What's up?" Dad asked, looking up from his computer.

I leaned against the door frame "Dad, I need to ask you something and I need you to be completely honest."

"I can try. What's up?"

"Those creatures, the ones that live in the woods, what are they called again?"

"I've heard them called many things, the most common, that I've heard, is annihilation."

"Is that something you could google and they'd show up?"

"If you googled the right question. Kate, what's this for?"

"Is that a made up word or an actual word?"

"It's an actual word, basically it means death. Why?"

"We're screwed."

"Excuse me?"

"Dad, if those annihilation are actually what's in those woods, they aren't harmless anymore. Dad, I think they might have found a way to be out in the open and not die twenty four hours later."

"What on earth are you talking about?"

"Dad, those are the only known ones in existence! I think they've evolved and found a way to leave the woods and not have to do it during the night."

"How much sleep did you get last night?"

"DAD! I'm not kidding. I think they're the ones who blew up the school and told everyone who you really are."

"I hate it when your mother is out of town."

"Please believe me."

"I try, I do, I just can't. Kate, I just don't think it's likely that it happened."

"So you don't believe me?"

He shook his head "I'm sorry baby girl, I just don't, not this time."

I left the room, went upstairs, searched my desk, grabbed the flash drive, grabbed my keys and left; might as well get back to school as fast as possible.

By the time I got back to school, there was really only an hour left. I ran across the field and joined my friends. "Hey guys, what'd I miss?"

"Not much. Where'd you go?" Kelly asked.

"I had to talk with my dad."

"What was so important that you had to leave school to talk with him about?" Steve asked.

"You're all going to hate me for saying this, I already hate myself for having to say it."

"What do you mean?" May asked.

"For the first time ever, there have to be secrets between the four of us. Before you protest, just hear me out. Look, I don't want to do this, but I think we have no choice. I've been hearing voices, a lot. It's never been like today, it's always been like it's my own thoughts, I never thought it was but I didn't know what to do. I think I know what they are, and I think Steve does as well."

"I want nothing to do with this."

"Just listen. As I was saying, May, you and Kelly haven't been hearing any voices. I think it's some kind of weird sign or something. My dad doesn't believe me when I told him that whatever blew up the school has evolved and is after something. I know that this sounds completely crazy, and all that, yet at the same time, it's the only thing that makes sense."

"Kate, hearing voices, that used to be seen differently than it is now. If you really are hearing voices it's not something you should talk about. I mean-"

"May, all those people within the past few generations that have been hearing voices, I know they've all gone missing. I promise you, I'm not going to go missing. We're going to be the ones who make it stop. I won't be able to do it alone though."

"If you can't do it alone then why would there need to be secrets between us all?" Kelly asked.

"We're gonna have to rely on how much we trust each other for this. We can't have a whole lot of communication between the four of us. Look, we're gonna have to do this is two groups and we're not gonna be able to work with the other group. This all relies on trust. We have to trust each other and believe that we'll be able to do everything we need to do. The groups, those have already been decided. It's me and Steve and May and Kelly. I don't think

Steve and I will be able to talk much about what we'll have to do either. It's gonna suck but, we have to do it."

"What are we getting out of this? I don't see anything coming out of this that'll be worth everything that we're risking." Steve said.

"I rather not be grounded the rest of my life." Kelly said.

"You're insane and this should be handled by the police." May said.

"I've tried telling the police, they wouldn't listen, they thought I was still loopy, and that was last week."

"If everything just clicked today-"

"Doesn't matter. It made sense to my Dad when I told him, although today he said I'm insane. Look, even if it didn't make sense to me then, if the police were going to take me seriously, they would have listened."

"Kate, I dunno about this, we'd be risking a lot."

"I know, and I know it's damn near impossible. Something's telling me that this is the right thing to do and, I wouldn't be able to live with myself if I didn't try. I rather die trying than not try at all."

The three of them looked at the grass. "We can't help you. I'm sorry, but this is just too insane and too dangerous, even for adults." Kelly said.

May and Steve said nothing; I took it as they agreed with her.

I got in my car and drove over to the park, I parked my car and headed towards the woods. If I ended up in Maine again, I ended up in Maine. I didn't know where I'd end up, and I didn't care. I still didn't understand how I even ended up in Maine last time, the woods were too small to even cross into the next town, let alone another state.

I reached the middle of the woods, everything started spinning, I lost my balance and fell. Round and round everything went, it lasted for hours. Over time, everything would change from bright and clear to dark and hard to see. I had no idea if it was the days changing or not. No matter how hard I tried, I couldn't close my eyes. I wanted nothing more than to be out of the woods and for everything to stop spinning.

All at once everything stopped spinning, everything was a whole lot warmer. I got up and started running. I ran as fast as I could, I ran to where I thought was the road, it was a dirt road, not paved and nowhere near home.

I walked along the road, I didn't know where I'd end up, I could only hope that I'd end up somewhere where I could find out how to get home. The sun had been rising when I started along the road, and was just starting to set now.

I smelt something burning, I sneezed, when my eyes opened I found myself on the roof of an abandoned building. I could feel the roof caving beneath me. It was too high to jump and be safe, I didn't know what to do, I didn't know where I was, I did the only thing that made sense, nothing. I wanted to scream and cry, I could do neither. I heard a loud cracking noise, I jumped out of fear.

I didn't land on the ground, I landed in a tree, not just any tree, the tree outside Steve's window. I started screaming, the window opened and Steve appeared.

"What the hell are you doing here? Sorry that was rude. What the hell? Nope, still rude. Where were you? Everyone's been looking for you? It's been a month."

"Of great, nice to know how long it's been. I don't know what's going on and I sure as hell wish I did. Everytime I close my eyes, even for second, I end up somewhere different. I think I figured out why those people have gone missing they've-" I blinked and I was gone.

I kept bouncing from place to place, never in the same place twice. No matter how much I willed it to stop, it wouldn't. That is until, everything started spinning, everything was spinning for only a minute before it stopped. I landed hard on the ground, at least it wasn't some place random.

"EVERYONE I FOUND ONE!"

"Come on, up you get." They held out their hands, I took them.

Once I was on my feet I realized who it was. "Please tell me I'm seeing things. I can't, I don't-"

"It's over, it's not gonna happen again. You okay?"

I couldn't wrap my head around anything, I could barely register that I was standing. "I, you, what, spinning, teleporting, insan-"

His lips met mine, he quickly pulled away. "I shouldn't have done that, with your parents hating me and all."

I stared blankly at him for a minute. "Trust me, they should be hating me, not you. I didn't listen when I should have."

"Do you remember anything?"

"I remember everything, even the things I had forgotten."

"How is that possible?"

"I don't know. I don't even know how I'm still standing here. What happened? How long has it been?"

"It's been three years. I promise, I'll explain everything, just not right now and not here."

I looked around, people were falling out of trees all around. "Why are people falling out of trees?"

"Like I said, I'll explain later. You okay?'

I nodded "I think so."

He cupped his hands around his mouth. "HEY EVERYONE! THEY'RE ALL OVER HERE IN THE CLEARING!"

I looked around, this in fact was not just any clearing, the old abandoned building stood behind me, it looked as if it had just been built. I'd only ever seen it this way in photographs, now it stood good as new in front of me.

I turned around and saw that people were coming towards us, I searched for my parents. I quickly spotted my father, I took off running. I flung my arms around him and buried my face in his shoulder.

"I missed you baby girl. I couldn't believe it when May told me. I feel bad for not listening to you, I think you're incredibly stupid, but I love you because you're my daughter and I don't know what I'd do without you."

"I love you Daddy."

"I love you too baby girl."

I pulled away and looked around. "Where's Mom?"

"She didn't come. She went looking yesterday. She's at home today, yesterday I was at home."

"Why is she at home?"

"You'll see. Don't worry, it's nothing bad"

"KATE!"

I turned around and took off running. "Kelly! May!"

I hugged them both. "Will one of you please tell me what the hell happened. No one's telling me."

"We would, accept Steve would kill us. Besides he knows more about what happened then we do."

"He was so pissed off, he'd become easily annoyed, he didn't want to do anything and all of a sudden he had this passion to solve whatever it was. I don't know how he did it, but he did."

"Just look around, everyone who's gone missing in the past two generation is popping up. Would it be falling up?" Kelly said.

I smiled "Maybe falling back to earth."

"That's what I meant."

The three of us laughed. "I'd really like to know-"

"If you want to know, I'll tell you, but like I said, not here."

"Then where?"

He looked at my best friends "You didn't tell her?"

"Tell me what?"

"Nothing."

I glared at them. "I swear-"

"Oh, just come with me. May-"

"I know."

Steve took my hand and headed towards the woods. "Don't worry, it's not going to happen again, we're just going over to the park."

I sighed "Ok."

We walked in silence, when we reached the park we crossed the bridge, we sat on the play structure. "What happened?"

He took a deep breath. "Well, after we said we weren't going to join you, you left. We all thought you just went home, it never occurred to us that you actually went to the woods. You didn't go to school the next day, I thought you weren't feeling up to it, that's what we all thought. I overheard my parents talking and I heard my mom say that you went missing. I told May who in turn told Kelly. The three of us didn't talk about it, I don't know if we didn't want to or if we just couldn't. When I saw you outside my window in the tree, I thought I was delusional, I didn't expect it, then you started speaking, I thought it was nonsense until you vanished into thin air."

"So you thought that me just popping- okay that does make sense."

"It took me a few days to actually realize what was going on, when I did, it hit like a ton of bricks. I begged my mom to look into it, she got so fed up with me bugging her that she and Justin worked on it when the could. It took about two and a half years before they could find anything. By the time they did, a lot of people had gone missing. It took six months for anything they tried to work. It sucked because it seemed like was impossible to do."

"What kept everyone going for that long?"

"It was different for everyone, for me, it was being able to see you again. Despite what you might think, it was the last six months that were the worst. No one was able to figure out how to get rid of them and make it all stop. Three days ago, a three year old, he had gotten away from his mother, he just started hitting them all, they were all burning up. They were burning up and not coming back. It was a mob of toddlers that killed them all."

"Really? Toddlers? That's insane."

He nodded "I'd been thinking about it for a few hours, it actually made sense. Everyone they went after, they between four and eighteen. The younger they were the more harmful they were to whatever those were. That's why adults thought we were insane, they didn't understand it."

"If that happened three days ago, then why'd everyone pop up today?"

He shrugged "Maybe because whatever they were doing lasted for twenty four hours before it'd stop. I say twenty four hours because people started showing up exactly twenty four hours later."

"Why'd the place go back to the way it was after? I still remember popping up in random places, and everything that happened after I started hearing the voices. I can now remember what I had forgotten."

"There's still a lot of unknown's. I think your dad wants you."

"I'll see you later." I leaned towards him and kissed his cheek.

"That's another thing we need to talk about."

I smiled "I agree."

"Kate come on! We gotta go!" Dad called.

I stood up and walked over to my father. "We going home?"

He nodded "Mom's gonna be very happy."

"You didn't tell her?"

He shrugged "She's been busy today."

Neither of us said anything after that. It wasn't until we got home that anything was said. I saw my parents had put up a fence again, there was one when I was younger but they took it down when I got older.

I walked over to the fence and peered over it, all sorts of small toys, and plastic structures were scattered throughout the yard. "Why are there so many plastic play structures in the yard?"

Dad smiled, but didn't say anything.

I followed Dad inside, I went to the kitchen, I was starving. Where my father went, I didn't know. I stopped dead in the doorway, everything was the same, except there was a little boy, no more than three years old, crawling on the floor.

"Mom!" I shouted.

She came tumbling down the kitchen stairs a moment later. "MY BABY!" I walked over to her and she flung her arms around me.

"Kate, I've been so worried. Dad and I, we all thought you were gone. We didn't know what happened."

"I'm okay Mom. It's over." I pulled away, walked across the kitchen and grabbed the little boy off the floor. "Mom, who is he?"

She smiled. "That's Ben, one of your twin brothers."

I stared blankly at her "I have twin brothers?"

She nodded "Yes, you have twin brothers. Ben and Chase. They're three."

I didn't say anything, I didn't know what to say.

Dad came into the kitchen, he was holding another little boy. I looked between the two boys, they looked exactly the same. "Are they identical?" I asked stupidly.

"Yeah, they are. Jen, would you say it's time?"

"We talked about this. I told you, we'd have to."

"What are you guys talking about?"

"Have a seat." Dad said.

The three of us sat around the kitchen table, my parents each holding one of my brothers. "Kate, before everything happened, Mom and I had talked about whether or not we'd let you be with Steve if that's what you wanted. Mom made a lot of good points, if you want you can be with him."

At first I didn't say anything, three years ago I'd have given anything for him to say that, now I didn't know. I knew that I'd find out, I knew a lot of things had changed and things would continue to change.

To be continued…

Printed in Germany
by Amazon Distribution
GmbH, Leipzig

20710883R00049